WALLACE HAS A HAPPY CHI

Text by James Drummond
Illustrations by Nick Hesketh

This book is dedicated to my grandchildren
Katy, Roslyn, Simon and Christiane with love.

The author acknowledges the kind assistance provided by
Strathclyde Fire Service during his research into
Wallace's history.

Other books in the series:
Wallace the Fire Dog
Wallace's School Adventure
Wallace Loses his Boots
Wallace and the Fireworks

© James Drummond – Text
© Nick Hesketh – Illustrations
Published in 1994 by
The Amaising Publishing House Ltd.
Musselburgh
EH21 7UJ
Scotland

031-665 8237

ISBN 1 871512 425

Printed & Bound by Scotprint Ltd, Musselburgh

Reprint Code   10   9   8   7   6   5   4   3   2   1

Wallace was a happy dog. He worked at the Central Fire Station in Glasgow, and like all working dogs he was happiest when he was busy. They called him 'Wallace the Fire Dog' and his special job was to go out with the fire engine, racing ahead of the galloping horses, barking loudly as if to say, 'Faster, faster! Out of the way everybody! We're in a hurry!'

The week before Christmas was the busiest time of year for Wallace and his firemen friends. Almost every day a fire would break out somewhere. Perhaps it was a guttering wax candle that set ablaze the dry branches of a Christmas tree, or a chain of paper decorations that suddenly flared in the heat of the gas light. And on Christmas Eve it sometimes happened that some child's stocking, hung up too close to the fire, would begin to smoulder and then burst into flames when everybody was tucked up in bed fast asleep.

Of course it was not all work and no play for Wallace, especially when the children who lived at the Fire Station were on holiday. This Christmas the favourite game was 'Doggy Tig'. You all stood in a big circle with Wallace in the middle and started to call out 'Hey Wallace' and the first person that Wallace bounced up to was 'het' and had to start barking and growling and chasing the others. And when you were tigged, that was you supposed to be bitten, and you became a dog as well and joined in the chase, until everybody was rushing about and barking and growling and snarling and one of the grown-ups told you to stop that noise or else come in to your bed.

What Wallace liked doing best was going out with the fire engine. In fact he did so much running about that one of the firemen made him two pairs of little leather boots to protect his paws from the hard cobbled streets. His other favourite thing was 'Doggy Tig'. The children could run really fast and when they barked they sounded almost like real dogs.

But they *weren't* dogs, and sometimes Wallace wished he had a real dog friend that he could scamper and tumble about with - like the black shaggy mongrel that for the past few weeks had been up for sale at the Ramshorn Bird and Dog Market just across the road from the Fire Station.

Three days before Christmas Wallace and his special friends Jimmy and Annie Paterson went across, as they often did, to speak to the Ramshorn dogs. As usual, there was a lot of friendly whining and sniffing and tail-wagging between Wallace and the shaggy mongrel. The market man was very gloomy. Business was bad. Nobody seemed to want to buy dogs for Christmas. If he didn't watch out the Dog Warden would be coming along to take away some of his dogs.

Jimmy explained to Annie that it was the Dog Warden's job to go round in a big van picking up dogs that nobody wanted and taking them away . . . . But Annie didn't want to hear any more about the dogs being taken away, and fortunately at that moment a noisy circus parade appeared at the end of the street. At the head of the parade came a troupe of clowns, handing out free balloons and leaflets that said, "Hengler's Circus – special Water Spectacular." Clutching their balloons, the children ran off to tell their friends about the parade.

They were in for a nasty shock. A queer looking van stood in the yard. The van was black, the driver's big hat was black, and between the shafts stood a black, rawboned horse with a tangled mane and a scraggy tail. "It's the Dog Warden!" exclaimed Annie. "He's come to take Wallace away!" "No," said Jimmy, who seemed to know everything. "It's worse - it's the Fever Van. Don't go near it or you'll get ill and die!" To her horror Annie saw that her friend Nellie was being carried out to the van by a very stern woman. Nellie was crying. The woman had a thin white face and thick black eyebrows. Behind her came an important looking man.

It's the Sanitary Inspector," said Jimmy. "He's a lot worse than any Dog Warden." The Sanitary Inspector slammed shut the door of the van with a dismal clang.

Poor Nellie had scarlet fever. Everybody at the Fire Station knew that. But they also knew that her mother had carefully nursed her day and night and that Nellie was getting better. She had been tucked up warm and comfortable in the press-bed in the sitting room, well away from the other children. The neighbours passed in bowls of soup and jelly puddings and kept it a secret that there was a child in the Fire Station who had scarlet fever. But the Sanitary Inspector had found out.

"This young female fever victim must be hospitalised immediately," he declared. "By my authority as Sanitary Inspector I order her immediate removal to the Fever Hospital. I will have no argument!"

From inside the dark and gloomy van they could hear Nellie's muffled sobs. She was distressed and frightened by all these stern people. Annie's father, Captain Paterson, was standing by. He knew how important it was that little girls with scarlet fever should be kept calm and cheerful.

He whispered to the children, telling them what to do. Then he spoke to Wallace. "Here, boy! Get your boots on. You're going to join the circus parade." When everything was ready he thrust a shilling and a big brass bell into the hands of the driver. "Here you are, mate. You know what to do," said the Captain. "Now off you go Wallace. Lead the way!"

As they swung out of the Fire Station and joined the tail-end of the procession, the bystanders recognised the famous fire dog. They clapped and cheered and shouted things like "Here comes Wallace!" The raw-boned horse tossed his tangled mane and swished his scraggy tail to the cheerful sound of the big brass bell. Nellie began to think that a ride in the dreaded fever van might not be too terrible after all. Even the nurse's eyebrows looked less stern and black as she watched the children dancing and capering alongside.

The only gloomy person to be seen was the Sanitary Inspector. He was very embarrassed by all this merriment, especially when he spotted in the crowd the posh young lady he was hoping to marry. She was scowling at him as if to say, "I thought I was supposed to be marrying an important Sanitary Inspector, not a clown in a circus parade."

At tea time Mrs Paterson had good news from the fever hospital. The doctor had said that Nellie was getting on very well. She'll get home by the New Year, he said, and then what she needs is to get built up with plenty of fresh air and exercise and with good things to eat like fruit and cheese. The very best thing, said the doctor, would be to send her for a holiday to the Seaside Home for Children at Saltcoats. But Mrs Patterson didn't think that Nellie's mum could afford that.

The other piece of good news was that, as a special Christmas treat, the Fire Station children were to get to Hengler's Circus and Water Spectacular that very evening.

Annie said that she'd rather visit Nellie, but it was explained to her that nobody – not even Nellie's mum – was allowed into the fever hospital. So she went to the circus and enjoyed it. But she kept thinking about her friend. She wondered if the girl in pink tights had been built up with a lot of fresh air and fruit and cheese. The two little ones, who had been allowed to come at the last minute to take Nellie's seat, fell asleep during the plate-spinning act, but they woke up in time to see the lion jumping through the fiery hoop. "I'll bet we could teach Wallace to do that," said Jimmy. Then he whispered to Annie that he had just had a great idea, but he wouldn't say what the great idea was.

The Water Spectacular really was spectacular. The Red Indian girl Minnie Ha Ha (who looked like the bare-back rider with brown instead of pink tights) was just about to be chopped by her deadly foe, but in the nick of time the water door slid open and a flood of water came gushing into the circus ring, bringing with it Red Eagle in his birch bark canoe.

"Tis Red Eagle, my brave hero, come to rescue me!" cried Minnie Ha Ha. Everybody knew it was the lion tamer with burnt cork smeared on his face, but it was exciting all the same. "That," said Jimmy, clapping enthusiastically, "gives me another idea."

Next morning Jimmy went to work on his great idea. "I'm going to teach Wallace a new trick," he told his dad. "It'll probably take all morning, but we'll hear the alarm if it goes off. We're just round in Sandy's back yard." Sandy was Jimmy's best friend.

Less than ten minutes later they were back, Wallace with his ears cocked up and his tail wagging happily. Jimmy was looking pleased too. "That dog's a quick learner," he said. "Come on Wallace let's show . . . ." But Wallace was bored with doing tricks that were too easy for a clever dog. After he had gone nosing right round the yard to see that all the firemen were doing things the way they should be done, he trotted over to the Ramshorn railings to visit his friend the black shaggy mongrel.

Jimmy's idea, as he explained to the other Fire Station children, was to stage a circus of their own in Sandy's back court and invite all the neighbours. They would take a collection at the end and might make enough money for Nellie to go for a fresh air holiday at Saltcoats. Sandy's mother said yes, they could have their show in the back yard just as soon as she had emptied the water from the wash-house boiler. Jimmy asked would she please leave the water in the boiler as he had just had another great idea? Annie started jumping about. "I know, I know!" she chanted. "A Water Spectacular!"

To begin with the back-court circus went well and the audience clapped loudly at all the different acts. Sandy clattered around doing a noisy clog dance on his stilts. Annie performed a few cartwheels in her pink tights, which unfortunately were a bit too tight in places.

But the star of the show was Wallace doing the new trick Jimmy had taught him that morning. Sandy said they ought to set the hoop on fire like in the lion's trick, but dogs are smarter than lions, and Wallace was clever enough to know that fire is a thing to be afraid of, not to play with.

Unfortunately Jimmy's Water Spectacular turned into a Water Disaster.

When the worst of the spluttering and shouting and complaining had died down, Annie tried to get on with the show. "Tis Red Eagle, my brave hero, come to rescue me!" she cried, hoping the excitement of the rescue would make the audience forget their own little troubles. But they were too busy wringing Sandy's mother's soapy water out of their clothes to bother much about what happened to Minnie Ha Ha. They didn't put much in the collection box - certainly not enough to get Nellie to the Seaside Home for Children at Saltcoats.

But there was enough to buy her some nice things to eat. "Build her up with fresh fruit and cheese," the doctor had said. And there in the grocer's special Christmas window display was just what the doctor ordered: two huge stacks of fruit, glinting and gleaming in the brilliance of Glasgow's first ever electric light display. And between the apples and the oranges – the biggest cheese in the world.

It was Lipton's famous Christmas Cheese. Each year it seemed to be bigger than ever before, and each year it was cut up and sold on Christmas Eve. It was a lucky cheese. In the piece you bought you might find a penny, or a threepenny piece, or a shilling. And for one extra lucky person, hidden somewhere inside the Christmas Cheese, was a gold sovereign.

This was the first time Wallace had ever gone on a shopping expedition. At first he didn't much like the gritty feel of the sawdust on his paws. And he was a bit worried by the whirring clinking noise of the cash-cups as they whizzed about cris-cross overhead between the counter and the cash desk. But he soon began to enjoy himself. There was a water dish marked 'dogs' at the entrance. And a very friendly assistant selling broken biscuits at knock-down prices to children. "Hold out your apron," she would say, and in went two generous handfulls for a farthing.

The best of all the grocer smells came from the cheese counter. Wallace eagerly followed the children as they joined the queue. If there was one thing that Wallace liked better than a bit of broken biscuit it was a chunk of Christmas cheese.

They waited patiently in the queue. But just as their turn came to be served they were roughly pushed aside. "You children wait your turn. We're in a hurry!" Wallace recognised the voice and growled. Annie recognised the voice and groaned, "It's the Sanitary Inspector." "And you," scowled the Sanitary Inspector, "are the young persons who have recently been in contact with an infectious disease. You should not be in a shop at all. Stand aside."

The rather posh young lady he hoped to marry giggled in a silly kind of way and looked up admiringly at her Sanitary Inspector. "You are so strong!" she murmured. "So very masterful!" The Sanitary Inspector bought her a piece of cheese.

The shop assistant saw what happened, but of course did not dare say anything to the Sanitary Inspector. So he winked at Annie, said "A Merry Christmas!" and gave her an extra large piece of cheese. Indeed it was so large, and Wallace had been so patient, she broke off a piece and gave it to him.

But instead of gobbling it up, Wallace sniffed at it suspiciously and tried to bury it in the sawdust with his nose. "You're being silly, Wallace!" scolded Jimmy. "Don't waste valuable food!" It certainly was valuable. Inside the piece of cheese was a bright gold sovereign. The Sanitary Inspector's young lady was furious. "If you hadn't been such a horrid cross bully we'd have got the Christmas sovereign!" And she burst into tears.

Of course Nellie's mother was delighted to get the oranges and the broken biscuits and the large piece of cheese. At first she said she wouldn't dream of taking the gold sovereign, but at last she agreed. "Thank you, children," she said, with tears of gratitude in her eyes. "This means that we'll manage a holiday by the seaside for Nellie."

When that was settled they all had a good laugh about their adventure in the cheese queue. The Sanitary Inspector was beginning to be a bit of a joke at the Fire Station. So when Sandy came in with the news that he had just seen him and his young lady going into the Skating Palace, the children decided to go and watch.

The children often went to watch the skaters through the back door of the Skating Palace. The machine that made the ice was old and rackety. Every so often it actually burst into flames, so the fire exit at the back was always kept open, just in case. If you hid behind the pile of soot and cinders you could listen to the music and watch the skaters without the rink attendant spotting you and blowing his whistle.

And sometimes, when he was away at the pay-box or having a cup of tea, you could sneak in and have a quick slide on the ice. Dodging the ice man was one of their best games.

Their enemy the ice-man was nowhere to be seen. In fact he had just gone down to the basement to see why the ice machine was making these funny noises. The children were about to nip in for a slide up the edge of the rink when a low growl from Wallace warned them that their other enemy, the Sanitary Inspector, was close at hand. Hastily they retreated behind the pile of soot and cinders. Obviously the posh young lady had forgiven him. "You skate so very well!" she simpered as they glided by. "I feel quite safe with your strong arm around me." Flushing with pride, and pleasure, the Sanitary Inspector shot off, skates flashing, to show how gracefully he could do a backwards glide.

Just at that moment, down in the basement the ice machine stopped making funny noises and burst into flames. A jet of hot steam went scalding through the pipes and instantly melted the thin film of ice on the skating rink above.

There were loud cries of dismay as skates went scraping and grinding into the cement floor. And cries of anger as the skaters tripped and tumbled and flopped down in the muddy pool that a moment before had been a smooth sheet of shimmering ice. The Sanitary Inspector's graceful backward glide suddenly turned into a clumsy and very uncomfortable backside glide.

It was a spectacular performance. Waving his arms wildly, the Sanitary Inspector slithered on his bottom the full length of the rink amidst a cascading spray of icy water. He made his final exit through the fire door and somersaulted head first into the pile of soot and cinders.

As he rose unsteadily to his feet, the Fire Station children hid behind some packing cases. "That," said Jimmy, "was a real Water Spectacular. I hope he's not hurt." "I hope he is," said Annie. "I hope he gets taken to hospital with a frozen bottom."

Only Wallace waited to watch him as he ruefully removed his skates and dusted the worst of the soot and cinders off his smart uniform. A bystander said afterwards that it was the first time he had seen a dog laugh.

But the posh young lady was certainly not laughing. "First you're a clown in a circus parade, then you're a big bully in a cheese queue. And now look at you – you are the dirtiest Sanitary Inspector I have ever seen!" And she flounced off, calling over her shoulder, "I never want to see you again." And she never did.

After all the excitement at the Skating Palace, Christmas morning seemed so nice and peaceful. Until Jimmy got back from the dairy with the milk and the rolls - and some bad news. "The black shaggy dog's gone! All the Ramshorn dogs are gone! Sandy says the Dog Warden came last night and he had a policeman with him and a big knife and he cut all the ropes and he shoved all the dogs into his van and the market man was shouting and the dogs were barking and growling and everything and he said he was going to take all the dogs away and . . .."

"Never mind that," Mrs Paterson interrupted hastily, seeing from the look on Annie's face that the tears were not far away. "Let's get this Christmas dinner on the go."

Annie pretended not to be too upset. She went bustling about, helping with the vegetables. It was the onions, she said, that were making the tears flow down her cheeks. Her mother said yes, onions were like that.

Then Nellie's mum came in with some vanilla tablet and stopped to chat. It was beginning to rain, she thought. The Santa at the hospital had given Nellie a little doll. And last night on his way home from work Nellie's dad had bought a dog to build up Nellie with walks and fresh air, just like the doctor had said. Quite a big dog. No, not any particular breed – a sort of mongrel. A black mongrel. By now Annie had stopped nibbling the tablet. "It's not shaggy, is it?" she asked eagerly. "Shaggy?" said Nellie's mum. She thought for a moment. "Yes, I'd say he was a shaggy dog."

The Fire Station children always went sledging on Christmas Day. There was never any snow, but the black slopes of the Sugarally Mountains did just as well. So after their Christmas dinner they all put on their very oldest clothes and set off, taking the black shaggy mongrel with them. Wallace had been called out to a fire in the city centre.

As they went sliding and slithering down the slopes on rusty tin trays and bits of old carpet, they shouted, "Gardey loo!" And when they lost their 'sledges' half way down, they slid the rest of the way on their bottoms, shouting, "Here comes the Sanitary Inspector!"

For Wallace this was just a normal working day. But he too was having a happy Christmas. A small candle on a large Christmas tree had started a fire at a well-behaved children's party in a smart city hotel. As the fire brigade dealt with the fire, the well-behaved children were ushered out into the hotel garden and told to play quietly. Wallace went with them. In the hotel they had played polite games like 'Pass the Parcel' and 'Hunt the Thimble'. Out in the garden games like 'Chase the Dog' and 'Throw the Mud-pie' were much more popular.

Soon the smart party children were as noisy and as dirty and as happy as the Fire Station children on the slopes of the Sugarally Mountains.

Playing with a crowd of children had been fun. Playing with a crowd of children and another dog was even better, especially when the children were you're special friends and the dog was big and tough and good natured and didn't mind a bit of a scuffle when you were both running for the ball at once.

As they scampered and tumbled about that Christmas Day, Wallace and the black shaggy mongrel were probably the happiest dogs in Glasgow.